T0298279

KIBBUTZ

SEAGULL
BOOKS
•
CELEBRATING
40 YEARS

THE FRENCH LIST

Shmuel T. Meyer

KIBBUTZ

TRANSLATED BY
GILA WALKER

LONDON NEW YORK CALCUTTA

This volume is part of a boxed set
titled *And the War Is Over . . .*
Not to be sold separately.

Seagull Books, 2024

Originally published in French as *Kibboutz*

© 2021 Les Éditions Metropolis, Geneva

English translation © Gila Walker, 2024

First published in English translation by Seagull Books, 2024

ISBN 978 1 8030 9 340 6

British Library Cataloguing-in-Publication Data
A catalogue record for this book is available from the British Library

Typeset by Seagull Books, Calcutta, India
Printed and bound by Hyam Enterprises, Calcutta, India

חומר חיינו הוא זהב החלוף היקר
הניגר אל גרוננו החם השוקק לחלב

*the stuff of our lives is the gold of transience
poured down our warm throats thirsting for milk.**

Meir Wieseltier

* Meir Wieseltier, *The Flower of Anarchy: Selected Poems* (Shirley Kaufman trans. with the author) (Oakland: University of California Press), p. 89.

To my children, Esther, Noam, Avital, Itamar,
Tehila, and Naveh

CONTENTS

KIKAR DIZENGOFF

I was a scraped-knees, shorts-and-sandals kibbutznik. I was at ease surrounded by rusty Massey Ferguson tractors and metal hinges, chicken feathers, and plucked oranges. I smoked, behind Motti's garage, my Noblesse pinched between thumb and index, without blinking an eye.

By day, I hated Meir who was with Tamar; at night, she came to me in my fearful dreams.

I drew the wounds of heroes on my shoulder. I was the child of a white tombstone a few steps from the orchard.

I knew the cotton *falh'a* of Yad Hana, its khamsin-scorched clouds of fluff, the slow-trickling green waters of the Nablus Stream, the dust track that led, between brambles and squirting cucumbers, to Abu Mussa's orange grove and his cinderblock hut.

I was a kibbutz pisher in my white Shabbat shirt and waxed shoes when Tamar took me to the terrace of Café Kasit to devour a poppy strudel.

She held my hand to cross Dizengoff Square.

From the cool, muddy pool rose, crepuscular, the croaking of frogs.

I was a hero from the kibbutz triumphing over Tel Aviv, June 10, 1952, when she kissed me.

ORCHARD BY NIGHT

I stopped the tractor. The sprayer's idling fan purred like a happy man, sated and stuffed to the gills. The night was cool, arrayed with stars in the treetops. A perfect night for the treatment, with a breeze so gentle it could hardly stir the frailest of branches.

I urinated on the rear wheel.

The floodlight cast mysterious shadows between the trunks and made the blue drops of poison glisten on the dented steel of the tank. The orchard breathed in deeply the tenderness of the night before the scorching of the day. I breathed with it the poisonous sulfur and the delicate air. Under the tightly packed terraced slopes, the moon divined the lights of villages and of sleeping cities beyond.

Without the fog, I would have seen the Shfela valley and the amber streetlamps of Kiryat Gat. Everything was so calm and beautiful that I could have grunted like a happy man, sated after a Noblesse with schnapps on a half-day holiday.

As I fastened the two mismatched buttons on my fly, my eyes followed the beam from the headlights of my John Deere and its scintillating trail of dust to the wide sewer pipe, a huge, tarred cylinder jutting out at the edge of the orchard.

In the grassy gap between the chaotic rows of peach trees, I spotted its thick shadow, its unsteady gait. A feral drunkard staggering like a baron leaving a brothel, tailcoat stained and wrinkled, eyes yellow, glazed, and fearful.

Opposite me, an eagle took flight.

To the brambles and the sun, little by little the dawn abandoned its ruffled tulle, like the skin of lukewarm milk along the edges of an old, chipped bowl.

The sky was bluer than the cold eye of a blind man.

Up above, motionless, a king, a hundred thousand times crowned, laughed at my fatigue and at the fragile happiness of this summer morning.

WITH THE LAND

We were up well before dawn. I tied the laces of my clodhoppers seated on the cooperative's milk crate. The coffee cooled on the concrete of the patio. You kept quiet. Quiet between and amid the stones. On white-moon nights, you kept the light shining on the vine leaves clinging to Rachel and Ury's house. Often, nothing stirred. You held your breath and the moon shone as sole respiration. Those who rise well before dawn know your fragrances. They jostle with nothing coming to disturb the natural order of things. First, the lawn that thickens with coolness, then the vine, again the vine that fills with all the vibrant heat of summer. When you lift the pure and biting breath of the desert upon you, the smell of chicken pens spiked with ammonia descends from the steps of Judea and, beyond, that of the fires lit in the village to feed the land with ashes and crystal.

And then you always keep me company, up there, toward the sheds. By now, our face is fresh, our eye sharp.

At my feet, my brothers sleep. Ury may have gone to the *falh'a*, as it's sunflower season.

I hear the crackling radio of the *shomer*, the watchman who makes his rounds, yearning for his bed, and the muffled tread of a stray dog who prowls, dumb and dirty.

Suspended upside down from the rafters, a strand of stationary bats.

The tractor seat, baptized with dew, is all brown moss and peeling plastic. I hold my breath as I turn the key, as if the fine mist from my lips and my swollen lungs could hush the sputtering of the engine. The headlights barge through wild grass and verges. When I climb down to open the twisted metal gate, returned long ago to its original rust, a frightened jackal abandons its prey.

Your orchard pulsates, resonates, dissonates. The desire for the peace of sleep mounts in me. Four Strauss lieder and the radio signal my presence to anonymous soldiers busy making tea bags dance in chipped cups.

In the white eyes of the tractor, the yellow eyes of dogs, gazelles, foxes, and eagles and the sky of mysterious constellations.

And in the distance, in the dark pricked depths of the wadi, the silvery shimmering of peach trees.

Never, my love, my beloved land, did I feel more confident, weak and powerful, than on summer nights when you kept me company, repeating on my lips "free man uprooted at long last."

SHABBAT CHOLENT

Gedalia was a brawny bachelor, a kibbutznik originally from Minnesota. He made up for his small stature with an unkempt goatee and a gruff disposition so antipathetic it guaranteed his continued celibacy for many a year.

Whereas all the other members of the kibbutz showed up disheveled, bedraggled, breath heavy from a warm bed abandoned with regret, Gedalia always seemed flawlessly fresh. On our night patrols, after nonchalantly tossing his weapon on the rear seat, he'd take the wheel of the jeep, slip a tape of his favorite group King Crimson into the cassette player and two hours would go by without a word between us. Two hours of driving through dark orchards, around coops where poultry clucked at every sweep of the headlights. Two hours of listening to a lousy progressive rock band.

With my Uzi carefully resting on my lap, I'd end up sinking into a state of lethargy more akin to hypnotic than to the borderland of sleep. He'd drive cautiously and, aside from the fact that he turned off the CB radio to avoid hearing the crackling idiocies of the army reservists coordinating patrols in the region's kibbutzim and yishuvim, Gedalia was someone who took his watch seriously, which was far from the case for all of the kibbutzniks.

A few nights before, the person assigned with me to protect the small perimeter of our country that adjoins our fields and homes managed to crawl out of bed only to fall back asleep. For the remaining hour and a quarter, he curled up in a fetal position on the passenger seat that he'd reclined to a sleeping position. And that was nothing compared with the guy who finally answered the door only to grab the walkie-talkie from my hand and go right back to bed, leaving me to keep watch by myself over the peaceful and fragrant borders of the night.

There were watches that everyone hated. The ones in the middle of the night of course that robbed you of your fair share of rest. But oddly, the Shabbat night watches were loathed most of all. Gedalia and I made the most of this somewhat atavistic loathing to swap a watch between ten and midnight on a weekday for one between two and four in the morning on the Lord's Holy Day. All too happy to avoid this unwelcome chore, no one bothered to wonder about the obscure reasons for our nearly jubilant insistence on switching our watches with theirs.

So, on Shabbat I would join Gedalia, who was as antipathetic as ever, for an evening of King Crimson and a scrupulous jeep patrol of the orchards, the coops (cluck-cluck), the barn, before cutting our rounds short by a good fifteen minutes to verify my silent driver from Minnesota's gastronomic assertion that "the best time to eat cholent is four in the morning." We'd park the jeep behind the ramp of the commissary and soft-shoe our way between crates and condiments through the dark and silent kitchens.

The two massive stewpots of cholent stood on top of two old metal sheets, which were themselves placed on top of the blue flames of the gas burners. Two large fatty and fragrant columns of tin covered with lids.

I'd take out two plates and cutlery while Gedalia lifted the lids and, in so doing, released the sweet confit scent of the meat and paprika. At the top, over the potatoes and pearl barley, were the long cylinder-shaped kishkes, barely browned by thirteen hours over a low flame, and the hard-boiled eggs with their already dark-marbled shells. Gedalia would fill the plates, forgetting none of the ingredients, and we'd go sit on the ramp, our legs dangling. The star-studded night and the howling jackals deepened our silence, and we ate thinking that "the four-in-the-morning theory" provided us with the finest recompense for our vaguely transgressive sacrifice.

We had a few wonderful years of Shabbat watches until the new bookkeeper reduced the kishke portions for economic reasons. Our late-night thefts must have become more noticeable and inevitably the night came (I recall it was raining cats and dogs) when, drenched and dripping on the kitchen floor, we discovered four padlocks securing the lids to the handles of the pots. Gedalia spat out a "Fuck off!"

So, there we were. It was over. The next day at lunchtime the pearl barley will be stickier than glutinous rice from Shanghai, the eggs will be more rubbery than a hevea tree and the kishke, yes, the kishke, freed like a jerk from its skin, will let its core stuffing spill out and everything will be ruined.

When we got back to the jeep, I turned to Gedalia and told him that it would certainly be our last Shabbat night together. That there wasn't a chance in the world that I'd put up with King Crimson without legitimate compensation, and I added, "Damnit, Gedalia, when you come from Minnesota, for fuck's sake you listen to Bob Dylan, not King Crimson!"

CHERRY TIME

The first cherry trees to be covered with white blossoms were on the plot adjacent to the kibbutz garage where Shimon, a two-time survivor of Bergen-Belsen and of the Battle of Latrun, grumbled while exercising his art of miraculous repair.

From my bedroom window, I'd seen the white roof of the Burlat orchard grow denser and heard the infernal buzzing of the bustling bees pollinating the trees. The fruiting had been late—it had snowed in late March—and so it coincided roughly with the migration of the passerines heading back north to Eastern Europe. I'd been informed of this by someone from the Nature Protection Society. He'd come all the way from Jerusalem to discuss once again what to do to protect our harvest without harming his little feathered friends who so fancied our fruit.

The young man, whose name was David, had the nice lilting accent of South Americans, and it took no more than a few minutes for me to learn that he was the brand-new son-in-law of Motti and Luz, from kibbutz S.E., both champions of organic farming and coincidentally my professors when I studied at the Ruppin Academic Center.

Already last year, Avi and I had taken the initiative of ordering a sufficient number of hoops from Aryeh, the blacksmith, to shelter the entire plot, when the time came, under a huge net. To cover the fifteen dunams, I had to mobilize a dozen members of the kibbutz, two Manitou forklifts, as well as two articulated boom lifts with legs like a spider. In less than forty-eight hours, the orchard resembled a huge cathedral, silent and peaceful, traversed by white rays.

The plastic mesh nets that we hoisted and sewed together at a height of over eight meters left us with long burns on our forearms and the high branches left scars on our faces. After hours of sweating and directly confronting the sun at the treetops, we stretched out for a good half hour on the carpet of decomposing petals, in the cool shade of the cherry trees under the tight mesh of nets that pixelated the sky and the clouds and all that streamed through them.

Avi, who'd spent nearly nine hours at the top of his boom lift stamped with the logo "The Negev Pruners," was the most flushed. His long, athletic body, stretched out and inert, made me think of an old illustration of Gulliver in a children's book. Up above our heads, an imperceptible puff of air made the net quiver, like the billowing sheet of a soothing and welcoming spring.

As it's impossible to trap more than a thousand trees under netting without ensnaring a few reckless birds, ravenous or foolish, David had supplied us with a dozen nets that we set up vertically between the rows like volleyball nets. Their mesh was so tight that our dry, gritty fingers caught in them, as did the tiny feet of the migrating passerines.

I came home exhausted from the long day in the treetops. My daughters were playing on the grass. During the meal that we ate in the communal dining hall where their mother was on duty, I explained why we'd set up nets to catch the birds. My eldest daughter made me promise to take them after lunch to see if the trap had worked. It was twilight, the time of day that's called Bein Hashemashot, literally between the suns, and yet everything still seemed luminous under the white veil, as if, in this spot, night was suspending its fall while revealing new sounds, like the soft mechanical drip-drip. The earth was finally releasing all its warm, moist scents.

Avital, who must have been six, was holding my hand, fearful and fearless at once. I can't recall if there were a lot of birds gripping the nets, but we cautiously released each one. I held a little passerine trembling and warm in the hollow of my hand and blew on its belly as David had shown me a few hours before. Under the down, its small rounded, panting belly was red like the cherries it had been pecking. Avital blew on the other bellies and laughed at their all-too-visible voracity.

Pending David's arrival the following day to ring, identify, and release them farther north, we put them in small cardboard boxes pierced with holes for the night. On the way home, Avital, perched on my shoulders, hummed while caressing the warm air, her arms outstretched to the sky, her fingers clutching clusters of cherries.

UNCLE YONA

Uncle Yona was aware that his designation—since it could hardly in earnest be called an election—as transport secretary of the kibbutz owed much to his respectable gray beard, and even more to the fact that the two stumps he'd brought back from the Sinai War had limited his mobility to a wheelchair and made him, from this standpoint, totally impartial. Having spent two-thirds of his life on the kibbutz, Uncle Yona was damned sure that this position, held by then for ten years, was by no means honorary and most certainly not a sinecure.

He'd lived through the time when the kibbutz had only a Chevrolet pickup, and a McCormick half-tractor, and neither was for private use. Now there were more than fifteen vehicles in the parking lot behind the Colbo convenience store. Not to mention the ones assigned to VIPs: one for the plant manager, one for the nurse that was shared with the neighboring kibbutz three times a week, one for the marketing director, and the jeep in which the head of security slept.

Fifteen cars for a hundred twenty-three adults and forty-five youngsters of driving age when the city, recreation, culture, and good times were less than an hour away by car, more than two by bus, nearly three days by train, and on Shabbat, more than a week's walk. That couldn't possibly be enough!

Yona owed his appointment to Dany's dismissal in the General Assembly. A young native, raised on the milk of socialism, he'd nonetheless conflated the collective and the private when it came to vehicle use. In so doing, he'd incurred the wrath of both the "higher nobility" and the "lower clergy": the generation of the founders and that of the rookie members. It was a common, natural alliance, all things considered, between the patricians and the asslicking plebs yearning for recognition from the founding fathers and professing allegiance to them.

On a visit one Shabbat afternoon, I'd found Uncle Yona busy on his patio working out the weekly timetable. He was grumbling while chewing on his unlit cigar.

"The daytime schedule is somewhat workable," he'd explained between two sips of coffee (I'd never seen Uncle Yona without a wet cigarillo hanging from the corner of his mouth and a chipped mug of coffee that he'd drink with tiny slurping sounds), "yes it's somewhat workable during

the day (slurp) when the priorities are clear-cut, first economic, then administrative, then the non-urgent medical
appointments, private affairs (slurp), those I can manage,
even though (slurp) there's always a shitload of unforeseen
events and . . . it's always during breakfast (slurp). . ."

At this point, a description of Uncle Yona is in order.
Though barely fifty, he looked ten years older and not
simply because he'd been wheelchair-bound for thirty
years. My mother—so his sister—said he'd always looked
older than his age, more mature, more tiresome too, by
which she meant more "serious" because my mother always
found seriousness tiresome, and her little brother incom-
mensurably so. Uncle Yona had been raised, like she, in the
tutelary shadow of Aaron Gordon, but whereas he was a
pure product of the kibbutz's ideological *nomenklatura* (and,
I must admit, although I'm not in total agreement with my
mother, he was a *bissel*, a tad rigid psychologically), my
mother, as soon as she could, had run away from this
"Rousseauistic jungle." Go figure what she meant by that!

"The *balagan* starts at 6 p.m. (slurp), even on
Tuesdays, the film-screening day! They all want to go to
the city instead, as if the food wasn't good enough here or
the movie in Tel Aviv was better than the one in the dining
hall (slurp) and don't get me going (slurp) about Friday
evening and Shabbat . . ." He sat up, looked me straight in
the eye for a long time as he searched for his lighter in the
pocket of the overalls which he never took off, even on

Shabbat, "because if God exists, he won't reproach me for wearing the clothes of man's redemptive emancipation." Go figure what he meant by that!

He relit his butt, clutched a big red pencil and, hesitating at times, he crossed out a dozen names on his list. Then, taking me as a witness, he said, "You'll see. . . I'll be entitled to a visit from that big shlemiel Tsvika . . . who'll come on Betty's instigation. Their nephew's getting married Wednesday evening in Beersheba, and they won't want to go with Yankel (slurp)."

"But Yankel is Betty's brother, isn't he?" I was surprised.

"They haven't spoken to each other in six months. Can you believe it? They spent two years during the war hiding out in a farmyard in Poland, in a hole no bigger than three square meters (slurp) and forty years in adjoining homes on the same kibbutz and now Betty can't travel for an hour with her brother! Can you believe it?"

There was as much irony as sadness in his rhetorical question.

"And you? How long could you put up with my mother?"

He answered me with a long slurp followed by a coordinated vigorous thrust of his arms to back his wheelchair away from the table with half a turn of the wheel. Every Shabbat during his term as transport secretary, he'd come back home after the communal meal in the dining hall on tables covered with white tablecloths for the occasion. And, while the others took their sacrosanct Shabbat nap, my uncle would spend a good hour and a half drawing up the weekly schedule, which he would tack that very evening at 6 p.m. to the corkboard at the administrative office, alongside the list of chores, patrol watches, and the schedule of committee and sub-committee meetings. We had a ritual when I came: we'd go to the stables and then to the workshop where he worked weekdays. Reduced at a very young age to a sedentary activity, he'd learned to repair things, and the building that was called simply the Workshop had gained a reputation throughout the region. For thirty years, people had been coming from all over to have a watch, a fan, a transistor radio, or a washing-machine motor fixed. Yona was the wizard who could salvage for you a Singer sewing machine from the twenties or Olivetti's latest electric typewriter. The workshop ran with five salaried employees, since no members of the kibbutz would have been willing to put up with his perpetual impatience for more than a few hours, not to mention his high demands which, when met (and they always were), could practically make you believe in miracles or at least in the existence of God.

The skill set required to run the Workshop, and which only Yona possessed, had spared him for thirty years from having to participate in the job-rotation system. Thus, he'd been able to rule over his empire with no fear of rivalry, with the possible exception of the one pathetic attempt by Yankele Frishman in 1964 when, having been elected to the kibbutz executive, the fool had tried to place the Workshop under the supervision of the factory. His attempt, motivated by fierce jealousy dating back to their years in the communal children's house, had fortunately been foiled. Yankele Frishman hadn't been quite as lucky as Uncle Yona. Hit by a Jordanian sniper in an alley of the Old City in Jerusalem, the reservist had fallen a hundred meters from the Wall and was one of the dead and forgotten soldiers of the stunning victory of the Six-Day War.

On our Shabbat walks, Uncle Yona could never resist stopping at the empty Workshop, turning on all the fluorescent lights, and circling through it with big thrusts of his arms and his wheels. I'd admire his ability to move around the confined space, filled with machines, work-benches, and desks, and smelling so strongly of sawdust, grease, and filings.

"Just think," he said to me, "I've been Secretary General, Treasurer, Regional Councilor, I was even almost a deputy, but never (slurp), I tell you, never has there been anything as maddening as scheduling these kibbutz cars! I've seen all manners of human ambition, jealousy, and baseness but there was always something larger than life about them, they had character, ideology, madness . . . now there's all this nastiness, this mediocrity, and what's it for? I'll tell you what it's for. It's for a car! All this human misery for a car! Can you believe it? They'd be prepared to kill me and worse still to kill each other for a goddamn car!"

The first rain, called *haYoreh*, had surprised the kibbutz in the middle of the Shabbat afternoon nap. Uncle Yona was dozing in his wheelchair on the patio by his bedroom. Pressed against his belly, between his thumb and his index, the old legless bachelor clutched a big dual-ended red-and-blue pencil. I'd arrived just in time to prevent the week's timetable from flying off, getting soaked on the lawn or caught in the branches of the grapefruit tree. Before putting an ashtray filled with wet cigarillo butts on top of it, I'd glanced at the two A4-size sheets taped together to form a horizontal spread. I could just picture Uncle Yona drawing the lines, adjusting the columns, the tip of his tongue protruding slightly as when he was fiddling with the tiny workings of a pocket watch or soldering the printed circuits of one of the factory machines. Shabbat was concluding in a sprinkle of rain and the air was filling with the strong late summer scent of jasmine and honeysuckle.

"Shavua tov!"

The expression used to wish me good evening took me by surprise. At the kibbutz, we tended to greet each other in the evening with *erev tov* or *shalom* or *'al'aan* or *hi*, but rarely did anyone use the formal "have a good week" that marks the end of Shabbat. It was Avidan Narkis. He and I had played together as children. We were the same age. As far back as I could recall, he was the darling of the kibbutz, the grandchild of Avrum, one of the pioneering founders of kibbutz Degania and an air-force officer to boot! Because he epitomized the ideal of the New Jewish Man, he had a standing free pass no matter what he did!

And then two years ago, without losing an iota of his hereditary immunity, Commander Avidan Narkis had done *Teshuvah*! He who was predestined to be a New Man, emancipated from diasporic primitivism, had had his own personal Mount Sinai revelation. Avidan Narkis, with his calloused hands, clear eyes, high forehead, and chest covered in medals, had found God! Now he wore a kippa and ritual fringes. Mornings he'd stand on his patio, for all to see, facing the sun, armed with his tefillin and draped in his prayer shawl. All this in a socialist kibbutz! And without losing any of his popularity and the fond respect that the kibbutz showed him.

"Good evening," I replied softly so as not to wake Uncle Yona. He, too, switched to whispering.

"I came by to ask your uncle to reserve a car for me for Wednesday."

"All day?"

"Yes."

Carefully I lifted the ashtray to pull out the sheets.

"Let me see . . . Hmm . . . Wednesday . . . yes . . ."

I moved my finger slowly across the column of days then to the line of reservations. The pages were slightly damp.

"Wednesday . . . yes . . . the Opel Rekord . . ."

"Great! You'll put me down?"

"Yes, but just for the morning."

"What?"

"All that's left on Wednesday is the Opel Rekord and only until 1 p.m. Ronit has an appointment in the city at 2:30."

I saw that Ronit's name was underlined in blue. On the top left was a color key: red for work, blue for priority medical visits. It was as clear as could be. Ronit needed the car for an appointment with her doctor, and it was doubly clear insofar as her pregnancy was so advanced that you'd have had to be blind not to see it.

I turned to him with a look of regret.

"So Ronit has a 2:30 appointment, which means you can have the car until 1. Does that work for you? Should I put you down?"

He looked irritated. Ever since he started wearing a kippa, he'd hold back his feelings but the bitter pout on his lips belied the gentle, mellow gleam in his eye.

"Okay for 1. I'll do my best . . . Have a good week."

"Have a good week, Commander," I replied foolishly.

I hadn't been back to the kibbutz since the accident. It had rained all night. That fateful Wednesday Avidan hadn't returned by one o'clock. Ronit had had to walk to the intersection to hitch a ride. An old Peugeot station wagon from a neighboring moshav had picked her up. Her benefactor, a young beardless driver, who'd only held his license for three months, had lost control of his vehicle. The car skidded on the wet surface, rolled over three or four times, and Ronit lost her baby.

Uncle Yona resigned from his position as transport secretary. I'd found him hunched over his workbench in the rear of the shop. The windowless room that served as his office was dimly lit. Uncle Yona slowly raised his head when I came in. The magnifier screwed over his eye made him look like a battle-worn one-eyed alley cat. For a moment, I thought he was going to speak to me. Finally, he'd stubbed his cigarillo in the ashtray, adjusted the light, and gone back to repairing a travel alarm clock.

Ronit and her husband had left the kibbutz a few months later, and everyone knew, my mother said, that the kibbutz had pushed them out. Nobody wanted to cross paths with their misfortune and their anger.

I didn't go to Avidan Narkis's wedding, but I was told that the kibbutz had made a good job of it and that the buffet had been ordered from a kosher caterer.

THE WRITER

She put her hand on the doorknob and felt the cold porcelain in the hollow of her palm. Her heart, her ever-so-small heart, was racing. The bolt was worn out, so the door swung open without her having to make the slightest effort, an effort that was part of the scene she'd imagined and that evaporated, and with it the cautious, apprehensive rhythm she'd intended.

The slight delay would have given Freha time to adjust the scarf on her head and rearrange the gray curls that tended to slip out of the fabric. The little confidence she'd mustered since her arrival at the kibbutz vanished when the door, softly creaking, opened.

Daniel had aged of course. His hair, too, was gray, but his adult face was that of his father. The same heavy features, the same fleshy wrinkles around and at the corners of his lips, the same stooped back, the same high-pitched voice. It was her son, her eldest, the one who'd left home when he was not yet fifteen. Her son Daniel stolen from her by the kibbutz and Ben Gurion with the honey of their corrupt ideas, her son Daniel who now spread monstrosities throughout the world about God's people and about God himself.

He was there, sitting behind his desk. When the door creaked open, he swiveled around in a cracked leather chair that must have dated from when radios were still called wireless, a chair like a generous palm of a hand. A backless chair that Freha noted would not have helped him straighten the natural curve of his back and shoulders that he'd inherited from his father, the curve of late-night reading by the light of an oil lamp.

Over forty years she had not seen him. It had taken the father's death for her to find at last the courage to put an end to a Kaddish that had been recited every year for four decades, to resuscitate Daniel from among the unburied dead and accept that he was now the famous novelist who authored ungodly books she'd never read under the name Dani Armon.

At present Freha recognized her son without recognizing him. She saw the fright in his eyes and the embarrassment in his gestures. Here they were, face to face.

The sixteen years between them had simply disappeared and the son was nearly as wizened as the mother and the son could have been her brother. Freha would have liked to hold him in her arms but everything about him seemed unyielding.

"What are you doing here?" his voice was uneasy.

"Your father's dead," she murmured with an accent that restored to Hebrew its Levantine origins.

He could have been mean and asked the old woman if he was dead like him or dead like someone who really didn't breathe anymore. He could have worn a sorry expression that would have made her feel that some filial sentiments were still alive in him, but he didn't bother. He turned his back on her to pour a glass of water from the pitcher that trickled onto his work table and quite brusquely handed it to this exhausted woman who must have walked from the Beit Menashe junction and was sweating profusely.

She drank the water in one go after saying the ritual blessing under her breath.

"It wasn't worth your time to come all the way here for that," he added brusquely.

"I didn't come for that, my son, I came to bring joy back to my eyes."

"Joy has to be earned . . . and anyway I assume you have a television. I'm on it often enough, so you didn't have to make the trip to feed your eyes."

She made no reply. Daniel didn't invite her to sit down. He simply took the glass out of her hands and went over to the small sink to put it down. On the marble countertop was a round lidless tin of Danish biscuits and a torn packet of Turkish coffee.

The walls of the small room that served as an office were covered with books. Freha felt a shiver of pleasure run through her at the sight of the entire Shas, the six orders of the Mishnah and the Talmud, on the lowest shelves under the window alongside a great many other bound books that could only be the living word of our great teachers.

"There's a shuttle leaving for Tsomet Menashe in ten minutes. It'll drop you off at the bus station just in time to take the 1:10 to Tel Aviv."

Since he wasn't looking at her, she refrained from answering him, from protesting that she'd just arrived, that it was hot. Daniel's taciturn severity, she, out of all people, knew where it came from. He was the spitting image of his father! Her lot in life for fifty-five years! She knew what it required of her, the submission and the suppressed tears.

Freha had left her moshav early that morning. The bus's rocking had lulled her until she reached the Tel Aviv station. She'd noted the directions on a piece of paper that she'd tucked under her watchband with the tickets the driver had handed her. She'd blinked her eyes when the sun rose, strong and hot behind the date palms and eucalyptus trees that stretched along the road. Then, shunning blindness, she'd closed her eyes. Old as she was, her thoughts had drifted not to hopes for the future but to a past so distant it had no real colors, or else those of the days when the muezzin woke the Jews of the El Jadida Mellah without resorting to loudspeakers. She'd seen passing before her eyes, in no particular order, her marriage to the father, the ramparts of her hometown where the ocean waves came crashing in winter, and Daniel, who must have been six, with his velvet skullcap and brown curls, reciting Midrashim and the Mishna to his father. And already his rebellious look and eyes filled with questions that the father wouldn't answer.

The Tel Aviv bus station was a maelstrom beyond her grasp. She'd never been there alone. The father had always guided her as if she were blind through the chaotic lanes where the intercity buses servicing the kibbutzim and yishuvim throughout the country were parked.

The stop for the 362 bus that would take her to the Beit Menashe junction was opposite the HaSharon Street falafel vendor. Numbers drawn in red lead paint on a roughly cut piece of cardboard, hanging from a no-parking sign, indicated the bus lines.

She had an hour ahead of her, but she was unwilling to move away from the cardboard and its number. The street was, despite the early hour, bustling with traffic unfathomable to Freha, for whom everything seemed disorganized. To kill time, she'd watched the passersby. One in particular intrigued her. A hulking man, whose imposing belly preceded him by a good half-meter, plodded lead-footed up and down the street no fewer than three times in an hour. She saw how he suffered, mopped his brow, stopped to catch his breath, arms akimbo like two handles on a large amphora. The falafel vendor had raised the roller shudder of his eatery. Freha was taken aback by the sudden smell of grease and brine that wafted from across the small street. By then the sun had cleared the top of the building opposite her and was streaming down to her sidewalk, setting the air on fire.

"Ya better sit yourself down, ma'am. If ya waitin' for the 362 or the 364, they're never on time. No point in standin' there and roastin' in the sun, is there?"

He'd installed a plastic chair of dubious whiteness in front of his kiosk. Without waiting to be asked twice, Freha accepted the man's offer.

"Herzl Obadia, at your service, ma'am," he'd declared in a joking tone.

She'd thanked him with a smile.

"A small cup of coffee?"

She'd declined politely. Freha was not stingy; she was simply not accustomed to indulging in superfluous pleasures. She'd had a cup before leaving and, though tempted to have another, she wasn't about to give in to unnecessary gratifications.

Herzl had brought her a glass of water and Freha had thanked the Creator and her benefactor in his grease-stained undershirt before she drank it. The bus had idled in the sun while the driver was having his coffee. "Never on time," Herzl had said.

Freha had seldom had the occasion to "go farther North than Hadera," as the lyrics of a popular song by the Yonatan Geffen went.

Daniel had never been an obedient child. Would he have been more so if they'd stayed in Morocco? Freha looked at the huge billboards that disfigured the roads out of the city. From all the places on earth, it was this blessed land that they'd chosen, this land that had swallowed Daniel into its bowels.

He was right. She'd watched him on TV at her upstairs neighbor Mira Abuhaseira's place when he'd received the Israel Prize for his work, late that afternoon on Independence Day. The father had refused to go up and when she came back down, she didn't tell him that she'd almost cried when President Katzir had given the prize to her son.

She hadn't read the books because it was useless to pretend that she believed in lies. Dani Armon had killed Daniel when he'd removed the *el*, the reference to God, from his name. He'd removed himself from the community of the Holy One Blessed Be He, the father said. Dani Armon had invented for himself a past as a pioneer, a kibbutznik, an Ashkenazi. His father had buried him alive, and his son had done the same with his origins.

In the gentle halting flow of life, some end up believing that tragedy no longer exists. After stopping at more than ten kibbutzim and villages, each more charming than the last, the bus left her off alone at the Beit Menashe junction at around eleven in the morning. She walked down the road lined with orange trees in late bloom toward her son's kibbutz. Less than a kilometer from her destination, a young charitable woman picked her up. A man in his fifties, possibly a foreigner, was in the passenger seat. He was sweating profusely under his long-sleeve starched shirt.

"Are you going to the kibbutz?"

Freha nodded.

"Family?"

She wiped her brow, adjusted the scarf that had slipped toward the back of her head.

"No, an old friend . . . "

She hesitated before saying, "Dani . . . Dani Armon."

The young woman in khaki pants wasn't very talkative. She pointed to the house assigned to the writer, which doubled as his office, before continuing on her way to what looked like the industrial zone of the kibbutz. The man who was sweating heavily directed his steps to the cemetery on the hillside.

It was a concrete cube on stilts surrounded by an unkempt garden with a rusty swing and a bike in a similar state. The three steps leading to the door were cluttered with flowerpots.

The door had swung open though she'd barely touched the knob. He was there, sitting behind his desk. Hearing the door opening, he'd swiveled around in his leather chair.

THE TRAPPIST

A coward in a kibbutz is a bit like a pedophile rabbi in an ultra-orthodox yeshiva in Bnei Brak: you may not know what to do with him, but you know perfectly well what not to do to protect the community's honor. And the old proverb about not washing dirty clothes in public takes on its full measure of lather, shit, ultra-gentle detergent, and dirty little stains that cling to the fabric itself.

In those days, the notion of cowardice was quite restrictive. A coward, roughly speaking, was anyone who didn't live up to the communal and military expectations of the socialist institution that saw itself as the Salt of the Earth.

Like other kibbutzim, Kfar Avraham was a proud purveyor of heroes, officers, strategic thinkers, and people who'd given their lives for their country, even though the small graveyard on the hillside did not testify to this as strikingly as the Kyriat Shaul Military Cemetery in Tel Aviv and Mount Herzl in Jerusalem where soldiers were laid to rest in *Tsahal*'s starry eternity.

So, what exactly was the charge against reserve sergeant Aryeh Misgav, son of Leah and Yeshua Misgav, both Palmach heroes?

But let's not jump the gun here. Aryeh was, until Wednesday, June 21, 1967, a brilliant boy, a hard-working, devoted socialist, a model son, a valued fellow kibbutznik. He was too shy to belong to the class of show-offs and charmers. War had torn him away from the Ruppin Academic Center where he was studying agronomy. A reserve parachutist in unit 55, Aryeh was among the liberators of Jerusalem. He'd witnessed the death of his comrades Mordi and Ethan, had had to empty fifty rounds of ammunition from the barrel of his brand-new Uzi. Had he any idea how many Jordanian soldiers he'd wounded or killed on Giv'at HaTahmoshet, Ammunition Hill?

So what exactly was the charge against reserve sergeant Aryeh Misgav?

He'd seen the Western Wall, with his eyes he'd seen it, he'd touched it, with his hand he'd touched it, he'd wept for it, with his eyes he'd wept, laughed for it, with his mouth he'd laughed. Then he'd slept, the night of June 7, he'd slept the sleep of the living, under Jerusalem's starry sky.

The war, as everyone knows, did not last long, neither did the fighting, apart from some skirmishes here and there with cells of fedayeen caught on the wrong side of the Jordan. In fact, there were more of these than people care to recall, and the popular anecdotes about the dubious combativity of our enemies, along the lines of "boots left lying in the Sinai during the Egyptian troops' hasty retreat," tallied with the history that was being written. So the idea that the Jordanians and the fedayeen did not attempt much during this messianic whirlwind belies neither the great history of the victors nor the anecdotal stories that circulate at wedding celebrations, parties, and banquets.

On June 21, 1967, Aryeh and his comrades were securing the Hebron area. Aman, Israeli military intelligence, was tracking down the forces of Shukieri and Arafat's Fatah. Aryeh knocked with the butt of his machine gun on all the doors that lead to HaMakhpela, the Cave of the Patriarchs. He didn't do it with the smugness of those in charge, even though the aim for him and his brigade was to track down holed-up enemy forces and ferret out weapons caches. Most of the inhabitants were frightened old women, old men with eyes white from glaucoma, and snotty-nosed kids. Aryeh Misgav didn't like what they were being made to do; neither did his fellow soldiers. They weren't policemen, God damn it! They despised the people from the Shabak who, speaking Arabic better than Gamal Abdel Nasser himself, stuck to their heels with expedient methods and the arrogance of Caesars.

In the small hours of the 21st, they had gone to sweep out Al Kum, a village, fifteen kilometers west of Hebron. Everything seemed unreal, the sleeping village like a body trembling with fever. Long before sunrise, the hens and roosters were walking noiselessly through the empty back alleys. There had been no call to prayer, yet the sole light that emerged from all the slumbering stones was a pale neon at the summit of the mosque. Even the jackals that were holed up remained silent along with all the famished animals, because the war was also driving the wild dogs to starvation.

The butt of Aryeh's gun knocked off patches of old green paint, exposing the rust stains of misery. In each room, open or forced open, old women, youngsters, old children, and prematurely old toothless men huddled together on blankets, piles of mattresses, and rugs, awaiting, haggard and scared, the barbarian invasion.

Aryeh could no longer stand the lamentations, the throat-ripping shrieks of the women when a young man over sixteen was found and dragged off, wrists tied, by the Shabak agents.

So what exactly did reserve sergeant Aryeh Misgav do that day of the solstice, that day of solar and divine flares, to turn into the coward that he never was before this derangement of the senses?

The report by the military prosecutor, which leaves no room for doubt about the sanction, simply states "deliberate desertion of duty resulting in the direct death of three soldiers in his company," with no further details. The penalty was reduced due to the fact that the name of Aryeh, son of Leah and Yeshua Misgav, figured among the first on the list of distinctions submitted to the General Staff for, "acts of bravery during the battle of Jerusalem and the assault on Ammunition Hill."

Aryeh was demoted, whereupon the army forgot his existence. Aryeh refused to leave Kfar Avraham despite all the efforts of our committees and of the head office. But that was his prerogative!

It has been ten years since I or anyone else has heard my younger brother speak a word or utter a sound.

A pact of silence.

He tends the kibbutz gardens. Ten hours a day, he plants, waters, prunes, fixes the swings, removes the crushed medlars and figs from the paths. Those who ignore our story think that Aryeh Misgav lost his mind in the war. Those who know the reasons for this pact with the kibbutz call him the Trappist.

I don't even know whether he hears us, any more than we were willing to hear him.

For ten years, I've avoided the path that leads to the monastic cell he built for himself at the foot of the hill where the water tower was installed, the concrete tower that feeds our homes and his silent garden.

GIDI

"It's a betrayal! That's what leaving here amounts to! I get that people elsewhere in the world don't understand that! But if you don't realize it, then you're no better than they are!"

She'd taken her most serious tone in uttering this declaration in the form of a definitive condemnation. Her deep, raspy smoker's voice echoed through the dining hall so forcefully that a tension took hold, the kind that you'd do anything to avoid at eleven at night, after a long day's work and two hours of palavering about the functioning of the poultry branch, the integration of two new members, the purchase of a new washing machine, and who knows what else, after all, I'd been dozing.

Henia—she was the one talking—didn't usually take the floor at general assemblies and so her intrusion into the evening's debate had taken aback more than one member of the kibbutz. The last item on that day's (or rather night's) agenda was expected to be approved unanimously in ten seconds without the slightest objection and, end of story, everyone off to bed. And now here was old Henia, who'd attracted no attention to herself since her husband Avshalom died a decade before, shaking up the assembly with her patriotic remarks.

The final vote concerned the partial funding of Gidi's trip to America. Gidon, whom everyone called Gidi, had completed his military service after nearly five years from the beginning of his service to the end of his mobilization because of the Sinai campaign. And during these five long, difficult years, he'd served the nation with devotion. He'd been wounded on the canal. They'd thought they'd lost him; the bullet had passed so close to his heart!

I'd always made a point of attending the general assemblies, even though, over time, the blah-blah and the many diatribes, often driven by old hatreds, wore me out. Even if these disagreements were to no purpose, as a member for twenty-five years, I figured that only ideological obstinacy could still save the kibbutz from decline.

The young people, especially my daughter, saw me as a wretched conservative who kept Kfar Avraham from joining the modern world.

"Where do you think you're living, Papa? You need to step outside your orchard from time to time. The world has changed! Even Tel Aviv has changed. When was the last time you went to the city? You never talk to anyone, just your trees, and you have the gall to make decisions about my life and other people's lives?"

In reply to Hadassa's tirade, I'd said that I was a member of the kibbutz for more than twenty-five years and that I was entitled to vote, just as she was. That she could exercise her right and end of story. I must have added, since I'm a "narrow-minded idiot," that I couldn't give a damn about what was happening in the world and even less in Tel Aviv.

It was stupid because I didn't believe a word I said. But I couldn't help it. I was seeing the kibbutz that I'd loved so disintegrating before my eyes and I had no intention of changing in any way my ideal, my dream . . . It was my life!

Hadassa was not an activist of change, but that didn't keep her from backing her husband, who used to live in the city, in Nahariya. She stood by his side and openly advocated for children to spend more time with their parents, even though, after six years of marriage, they had yet to make me a grandfather. I had a hunch that my daughter was ready to hammer the first nail into the coffin.

Henia's remarks made my neighbor leap up in rage, which triggered a chain reaction that ended up getting the better of my sleep.

"What the hell, Henia!"

Henia was now scowling in her seat in the corner. Only her arthritis-crippled fingers still seemed alive as she drummed on the table.

In over twenty years, I'd never heard the sound of her voice in a general assembly. This little wisp of a woman, wizened by the years and the sun, was discretion itself.

A long time ago at her daughter Ilana's wedding (Avshalom, bubbly and charismatic, was still in this world at the time), we'd had the occasion to talk, I mean to exchange something other than the commonplaces of day-to-day communal life. Henia was a highly cultured woman. Born in Prague at the end of the nineteenth century, she'd been a brilliant physics student in Berlin before meeting Avshalom, the Palestinian representative of *Hashomer* in Europe. They'd moved to *HaAretz* in 1932.

"When we made aliyah, we came straight to kibbutz Kfar Avraham . . . You simply can't imagine what it was like to go from the lap of luxury on the Ku'damm to a damned backwater infested with mosquitos the size of my thumb (she demonstrated with her finger). It was like . . ." She couldn't find the words to describe the downfall, or was it rather a glorious accomplishment? Hard to say what the pupil of her eyes expressed that night.

"What the hell, Henia!"

"Yes, Henia, really. . . What do you mean? Are you saying that you're against funding Gidi's trip?"

It was Secretary Itzik who followed through on my neighbor's "What the hell!"

Henia, in her corner, kept quiet.

My son-in-law, who I repeat was not born on the kibbutz, felt justified in going on the offensive.

"I think that fellow kibbutz member Henia hasn't really understood that this is not the first time that the kibbutz is financing an individual project. Didn't you yourself, Henia, benefit from kibbutz funding for four years of Bible studies? Gidi's project which, you will admit, is well deserved, is to go spend a few months in America. Is it that you don't like America? Well, I don't particularly like Bible studies."

Approving yeses resounded from all sides, like ayes in the House of Commons.

It was always the same people who spoke up, exerted influence, took vehement stands and, ultimately, made the decisions. Avshalom used to be one of them. Henia, on the other hand, had always kept her thoughts to herself.

For my part, since my ouster from the Executive Committee about ten years earlier, an ouster that had left a bitter taste in my heart and mouth, I would show up, not take part in discussions, make up my mind, and vote.

By now my neighbor was beginning to foam at the mouth and everyone was speaking at the same time, a racket amplified by the tarred corrugated panels that served as a ceiling. The members were talking among themselves and had forgotten Henia's very existence. It felt so wrong to abandon the old woman to her anger that I decided to defend her, even though I had nothing personally against financing a round trip to the moon, if that's what Gidi desired. I was fond of this straightforward, solid guy who I'd secretly hoped would have married Hadassa.

By challenging my son-in-law who was doing a splendid job of playing the role of a "modern" offended by the revolting resurgence of conservative thinking, I triggered stunned silence for the second time that evening. It had been so long since I'd spoken at a general assembly.

"You must be telling yourself that your remarks were well put. You're pleased with yourself, are you? You figure your argument was so intelligent, so well turned that it didn't even make you blush to throw in Henia's face that being a tourist in New York or in Hollywood is roughly the same as learning to understand the Bible. She's right. Henia was right even before you opened your mouth. I'm not saying that Gidi doesn't deserve for the kibbutz to help him get his feet back on the ground, he thoroughly deserves America and probably more. What I'm saying is that the kibbutz doesn't deserve to self-finance its own demise!"

Since no one interrupted me and Henia's eyes were encouraging me to continue, I took the risk of veering off topic.

"What will be left of Kfar Avraham? Of socialism or equality? Of the Zionism that made us choose to live here rather than in America or Uganda? What is left of us if we see Bible studies as a joke? We draw our ideal from these stories that you denigrate, not from riding on the Coney Island Ferris wheel in a Hawaiian shirt!"

I'd spoken without bothering to stand up. Seated at my side, my neighbor stared at me, eyes wide open, as if she were discovering me for the first time, as if I hadn't existed before opening my mouth.

I half-expected her to yell her "What the hell!" again and readied myself to meet her rage by tensing all the muscles of my body, as if she were going to punch me in the shoulder or worse.

As she remained speechless and my son-in-law hadn't yet summoned up the clever words that would surely make me look ridiculous, I took the opportunity to make my getaway. No one thought of holding me back. They'd vote without me and without Henia who'd preceded me with her sturdy step.

The night was tender as it is sometimes though very rarely in the spring. It was so full of mingled scents of orange blossoms and jasmine that it lazily crushed the kibbutz, like a large milk-filled breast, a baby's cheek.

I caught up with Henia soon enough since she'd slowed her pace.

"Thank you."

"For nothing, Henia . . . You know that I have nothing against Gidi who must be the best of grandsons."

"Yes," she replies, "the best grandson."

Our paths parted. She headed to the infirmary and I to the children's homes.

I did not go inside straightaway. I wanted to take advantage of this perfect night, full of stars, shiny as a new oilcloth. Utter silence reigned in the vicinity of the children's homes, the silence and coolness of the giant eucalyptus trees planted forty years before by Henia and Avshalom and all those to whom the kibbutz nowadays listened no more.

*

That was ages ago. Children now live with their parents. The kibbutz built three districts of small two-story apartments, like in the city. The brand-new dining hall is empty in the evening. Members have dinner at home with their family.

I'm still not a grandfather and I'm not about to be. Hadassa is divorced. She's living in a room not far from mine and my former son-in-law moved to England. As for Gidi, he never came back from the States. It seems he found a good job.

LA VIE EN ROSE

The story I'm about to tell you took place three kilometers from the kibbutz if you cut across the fields and five if you follow the hill along the path the Bedouins take.

I heard it from my grandfather who was someone important, a minister, I believe, for a time. He'd acquired a paternalistic sympathy for Albert and his family. The fact that I ignore Albert's family name may seem surprising, or it may be a clear indication of what those days were like, a political and social adventure for some, whereas for others . . .

When Albert came from Morocco with his family in the late fifties, they didn't know that they'd been tasked with the mission of repopulating the Negev desert. At the time, Ben Gurion's grand demographic dream boiled down to a score of tarpaulin tents and a prefabricated building on stilts.

The village, tentatively given the bucolic name of M23, was located some twenty kilometers southeast of Be'er Sheva. Beyond the fences and watchtowers, wind, broken rock, and, as far as the eye could see, flat, gray mounds mottled with dry brambles and skirted by exhausted wadi beds.

The Jewish Agency, in a carefully drafted agriculture development plan, had allotted the equivalent of one hundred dunams of land to each of the sixteen families, plus five hens, a roll of wire, and pliers to build a coop.

Albert arrived by truck with his wife Sima and his three sons. After the DDT in a shack in the Ashdod port, officials in khaki shorts had peppered them with recommendations in the form of threats and threats in the form of recommendations. They'd never answered the only question that really mattered to Albert: When would they get to Jerusalem?

At ten in the evening, after seven bumpy hours, the red Renault truck left them here, in the Negev. Albert had been the first to climb off the truck bed, leaning heavily on the wooden posts. He'd hiked up the legs of his suit, unfolded his red-checkered handkerchief, placed it on the ground, kneeled with affection, and kissed the sand while saying the blessing for special occasions: Blessed are You, our God . . . yadda, yadda. . . who has granted us life, sustained us, and brought us to this moment.

Then, using his right hand as an eye shield, he peered for many long minutes into the pitch-dark night looking for the outlines of the Tower of David, the crenellated shadow of the walls of Suleiman the Magnificent, and Zion Gate. His disappointment was immense at the break of dawn to discover a plain riddled with sand and gravel stretching to the edge of the horizon, and that, of course, no King's tomb, no hallowed synagogue, no Holy of Holies inhabited this desert.

The first winter was dreadfully rainy and M23, which had found at last a topographic identity and was now called Sha'ar HaKatzir, turned into a horrendous mud field with water gushing from all directions.

Of the sixteen families, only half remained. Maybe it was the language barrier or a different conception of husbandry. Whatever the case, it took less than six months for seven families to drop out of the game. Some families had feasted on a tagine every Shabbat and holiday and found themselves with an empty coop. One couple from Meknes, older in combined age than Methuselah, had experienced some difficulty tilling the soil to sow the seeds provided by Mishmar HaNegev's agriculture commissioner Gideon Blumenkrantz who, sparing in introspection though he was, nonetheless confessed to a faulty evaluation of "human material."

It wasn't until the middle of the following decade that Sha'ar HaKatzir became an official moshav, a collective farm. Albert and his three sons bravely put their shoulders to the wheel and the farm, gracious me, somehow managed to keep alive a family that had expanded to include three daughters-in-law and six grandchildren.

In place of the mud, Albert planted a jasmine arbor and two grapefruit trees that were supposed to be orange trees. A mistake at the nursery, admitted agriculture commissioner Gideon Blumenkrantz, who secretly nursed ambitions of being appointed to the Central Committee of the Party.

In place of the coop that didn't bring in a single penny, since the prices of poultry were not adequately supported by the cooperative or the government, Albert staked everything on dairy farming and, with the help of his sons, he turned seven starving cows into a herd of thirty Holsteins, stunted and stupid with teats swollen with milk.

After Albert's death, smack in the middle of an evening milking, his two eldest sons, who had other jobs besides farming—one on Negev's Regional Council and the other as a mechanic at the dairy cooperative—left the youngest son to manage the livestock and their father's debts: a pile of cardboard folders carefully stowed between two of the mother's books of Psalms that she no longer used since their bindings had come undone.

A visitor unfamiliar with the habits and customs of Sha'ar HaKatzir might construe this storage area as expressing the father's desire to create a Genizah, a repository of the holy and the profane in his home. But nothing of the sort. In fact, it was the mother's idea to place the two books of Psalms on either side of the debts hoping for their miraculous intervention in the family's calamitous financial situation.

But nothing worked. Not the photo of the venerable rabbi of Netivot nor the prayers of the mother. The farm, in debt up to the horns of Suffa, their last primiparous cow, was slated to be transferred by the cooperative to new farmers. That is when an idea occurred to the youngest son that hardly garnered unanimous support at the moshav.

"Why don't we turn the huge shed on the side of the road to Be'er Sheva into a Paris-style cabaret? There isn't a place from Cairo to Tel Aviv for us to go for entertainment. Dominos are all we have."

This was the argument, give or take a word or two, that Albert's youngest son made to the cooperative members.

To everyone's surprise, Gideon Blumenkrantz, the spirited deputy representing the moshav and the Negev at the Knesset, was the project's main advocate. Like Albert's youngest son, the politician was a devotee of the French *chanson*: Georges Brassens, Yves Montand, Piaf, and so on.

The two men combined their forces, went campaigning, challenged coalitions and conservative attitudes. Proud of the modernism that made dark reactionary spirits tremble, and energized by it, Albert's son and Gideon Blumenkrantz were victorious in the end.

Nine months later, on September 28, 1966, on the eve of Sukkoth, between Albert's former coops and the dusty Be'er Sheva–Dimona route, the first Paris cabaret in the desert opened its doors. The event caused quite a stir in the country. People came from all over, from Tel Aviv, from Jerusalem, from Sde Boker, and even from neighboring Bedouin villages.

The poster, in black and white, was understated. Designed by a Belgian artist, a volunteer at kibbutz Mishmar HaNegev, it represented a woman in silhouette, slender and curly-haired, readily recognizable to anyone who knew the lyrics or even the melody of the "Little Sparrow's" most famous song. The stylized representation was surmounted by an elegant *La Vie en Rose*.

The opening took place under the prestigious patronage of Esther Ofarim. Carmel 777 brandy flowed freely. Toward midnight, Albert's son, accompanied on the guitar by a German volunteer from kibbutz Mishmar HaNegev, sang "Les Copains d'abord" with tears in his eyes. On May 15, 1967, on the stony mound overlooking the junction of the road to Be'er Sheva and the now-paved road to Sha'ar

HaKatzir, Albert's son planted a poster that, to this day, no hiker could miss.

On June 7, that same year, the youngest of Albert's sons burned to death with two of his comrades in the hull of his tank. Vice-minister of Agriculture Blumenkrantz delivered a moving eulogy in the military cemetery of Mount Herzl.

The moshav collapsed irremediably. Leaving this poster on a billboard in the middle of the desert and a white gravestone under the Jerusalem sun.

FIGS

Divorces on the kibbutz are sometimes settled by a move to the other side of the drive. When my parents separated, nothing much changed for me, since the only meal I used to eat with them was on Shabbat in the communal dining hall. For those who are unfamiliar with kibbutz ways, the kids are raised together in dedicated homes where they sleep and play; they see their parents only after work—a "five-to-seven" that I've always considered the most trying time of the day. There'd be no story to tell if it wasn't for the fact that the drive that separated my mother's bedroom from her ex's (she's the one who decided to ditch my father) was one of the shortest in Kfar Avraham. I knew every concrete paving block that composed the kibbutz's most sinister mosaic. I knew every detail, all the cracks, the weeds, the brambles, the traces of crushed figs. My mother's crib was at the top of the drive and my father's at the bottom, with no more than seventy meters between the two, bordered by an untended lawn and uncommonly huge fig trees. Planted by a monomaniac dickhead twenty years earlier, the four humongous trees disgorged sticky worm-infested fruit in summer. In winter they clawed the air with their immense witch limbs, dark and gnarled, and armed with nails and swords.

My parents were hippies in their day. My father still collected John Mayall and Grateful Dead LPs and my mother made art from salvaged materials. He was a Sabra, a child of the Zionist aristocracy, and she, a German, more shikse than Maria Magdalena, minus the cross. Then again, my mother did have a cross of sorts, the one she bore to redeem the crimes of my grandfather, a Nazi dignitary.

I'm the only kid in this kibbutz who's as fluent in German as in Hebrew. My German is reserved for my *Mutti* and for Pintchy, who's in charge of the volunteers, and who, legend has it, learnt the language of the blondes in a horizontal position.

Pintchy was too young to have screwed my mother when she came to Kfar Avraham in the late sixties. The guy who scored with Ingrid the *Germanya* was the playboy of the hour, the lady killer of the pool, the local Robert Zimmerman, meaning Adam Regev, my father. Ingrid was one of a kind and, for the kibbutz studs, seducing her must have represented the ultimate trophy to add to their resume, alongside their stories of fighting in the Suez, in the Golan, or in Ramallah. But it was on his eternally faded blue work shirt, amply unbuttoned to reveal his tanned chest, that Adam Regev had hung the medal of Great Predator.

Was screwing a Jew Ingrid Castorp's way of killing her father, redeeming her country's soul, and overturning its history? Was screwing a German shikse the ultimate fantasy of regained dignity for the Jewish New Man? That was a rhetorical question that must have been going around my mind at the age of seven when I picked an overripe fig and hurled it as hard as I could against the yellowish stucco of the room where "Nimrod" of the pools lived.

Adam Regev had knocked up an eighteen-year-old, dazzling as a blue summer dawn, a child, an offspring of degenerate Prussian gentry, a pale, living grace.

It could have been one more commonplace story of sexual attraction between a foreign volunteer and a Levantine hippie, a tank driver in wartime and a chick fattener in everyday life. A pleasant enough story, as there were ten a year at kibbutz Kfar Avraham, which a passing volunteer had nicknamed the "fuckdrome."

They had a rabbi come from Tiberias, with a big belly under his caftan and a flap of his dirty shirt sticking out of pants scrubbed to the point of transparency. The rabbi signed three pieces of paper, talked for five minutes with my mother, and I became a Jew even before I was born.

The wedding was fittingly celebrated with schnitzel, Waldorf salad, and Dad on the guitar singing "The Times

They Are a-Changin'." I can't tell you any more about it because even though I was there, fetuses don't retain much of what they know about the world and its future woes.

I was never truly happy until the kibbutz agreed, at my request, to send me to board at the Kadoorie Agricultural High School in Lower Galilee. It seems I slept in the same dorm as Yitzhak Rabin. At any rate, I slept. Which was what mattered most to me and to everyone else.

The father didn't speak a word of German and never had the intention of learning it. His language was rugged and earthy, an extension of his tank and of his sex, certainly not the language of Goethe. My mother, on the other hand, had the accent in Hebrew of our greatest poets. Still today, I read Tchernichovsky, Alterman, Bialik, and Agnon with her voice.

The chicken fattener knew all the useful words of his language and was the product of a national whole, whereas his young wife was nothing but an exclusive spark, a particle, a collateral victim of the world's moral breakdown.

Forty years have passed, and I'm as old as both their ages added together, a tax added by the great scientist in the sky. I've lived both their lives and done nothing with any of it, at any rate not more than they did. Mama killed her favorite Jew before exploding her own head like a fucking fig on the kibbutz's ugliest and least well-tended drive.

ODESSA

In memory of Ivan Nikitin

When Ivan returned from Odessa where he was running a small Yiddish theatre, he told me about his walks through the city in search of that Jewish soul that would float in the air like a whiff of kerosene and lilacs and wild roses. He'd searched in vain for the last address where my parents lived, photographed facades for me and vestiges of synagogues converted into workshops, boutiques, barns, or factories.

"You're ghosts. I can sense you everywhere without seeing you. No city in the world is as Jewish as Odessa!"

Ivan was a poet and playwright in exile in France. I'd crossed paths with this Russian Orthodox, steeped in icons and wax candles, at a première at the Gesher Theater in Jaffa. He was a great poet, known by virtually no one except René Char, and I was now working on translating him into Hebrew.

La petite neige and *Aux confins de l'embellie,* a couple of his French books of poems had been quite well received and the leftist Zionist newspaper *Al' Hamishmar* had published some excerpts in its Saturday supplement.

Ivan loved to come to Kfar Avraham. He'd sit in my office, run his hand over the books on the shelves, look for the right place and, once he'd found it, he'd insert the book he'd brought back for me from his travels. Little by little, my library was enriched with books on the most beautiful icons of Saint Nicholas the Wonderworker, Gogol, Mandelstam, Yitzchak Lowy, and Babel, of course.

Ivan was as fair and frail as I was dark and burly. He was as rooted in falsehood as I was uprooted from truth.

Each of his stays, which never lasted more than two nights, was an orgy of vodka. Ivan was not only melancholic, but he was also in despair. Recently, custody of his son had been taken from him and his teaching position as a professor of Russian literature in France was uncertain. Ivan drank, recited Pushkin, wept, laughed, recounted his latest love affair with an Argentinian singer, unclear as it was whether it was a happy or unhappy story, and fell asleep in his undershirt, collapsed on the sofa intoning "Me Vuelvo."

His sleep was never deep, as if he were giving himself over to his dreams alone. His eyelids quivered with what his inner eyes were seeing. When I woke that morning, despite the very early hour, I found him busy preparing two cups of instant coffee.

"I'm quite certain that only on the kibbutz, at your place, am I willing to drink dishwater . . . Mind, I don't hate it and . . . I'd even be tempted to say that I appreciate it . . . the land of miracles that is yours (then, in a low voice), a land of destiny, abysses, and dreams that is mine."

Turning to me, he burst out laughing as he wet his whistle with his first glass of alcohol.

The day was studious. We worked on the translation of his latest book of poems. My Russian was academic, and Ivan unbound it for me. I liked his verses which sounded like an impassioned Mussorgsky or a penitent Rachmaninov. I wanted to render the same texture in Hebrew. We were working that day on a prose poem. A tightly crafted text, compact like a railway convoy whose end you desperately await. A musical monotony, like the sad rolling of wheels and axles in a countryside of ice, remote forests, and suspended life.

The story was about two couples whom Ivan had known a very long time before—Zalman Altshuler and Nina Malamud, and Sasha Bagritzki and Elina Apukhtin. Inseparable since their days at Kiev University, they'd become specialists of Russian theatre and divided their time between teaching and research, until the day that Zalman and Nina were expelled from the university for Zionist cosmopolitism. After a year without really working, the Odessa highways department refused to hire them. As for the rare publishers who had still accepted their writings, they'd fired them without pay.

At the end of two years, they'd applied quite pointlessly for a visa to Israel, naturally refused, but which led to their eviction from their room on Sadova Street and their expulsion to the dark outskirts of Moldavanka.

It was Elina who came up with "the solution," simple and awfully uncertain. The idea was for the couples to swap partners, get married for the time it would take to get a visa to go abroad. A mixed couple, thought Elina, and Zalman who immediately agreed, was neither fish nor fowl, and order detests nothing more than uncertainty. Would they have a better chance of escaping Soviet rigidity if they registered outside Ukraine?

This was the case for Sasha the Ukrainian and Nina the Jew, who were granted the right to leave for Vienna two years after submitting their application, but unfortunately not for Elina the Russian and Zalman the Jew.

Nina and Sasha went into exile in Israel, waited a long time for letters from Elina and Zalman that never came, and only seven months for the birth of the child Nina was carrying from Zalman. Five months after Sasha's departure, the Odessa marine police found Elina's half-floating body on a beach in the south. Nina remained without word from

Zalman until the Glasnost. That's when she learned, through friends who'd recently arrived in Israel, that my father had died in September 1973 a few months after he arrived in a camp in Eastern Russia. I was six months old, and my mother had placed me in Kfar Avraham.

Ivan's eyes were wet with alcohol, sweat, and tears.

"Your coffee is downright disgusting, Saul Altshuler!"

THIRD'EAR

I too had a cat, in fact I've had two, although "have" is hardly the right word to describe a relationship to a cat. First there was Maizena, when I was a philosophy student in Paris in the mid-seventies. Black, shiny, and elegant like the coal of Galicia. I left for Great Britain and left her to a long life of plutocracy on the family estate (eating veal liver, watching *Des chiffres et des lettres*) and thereafter to an accidental death on the Côte d'Azur. Age-related no doubt. A grave under the cypress at the foot of the rock garden that marks the beginning or the end of what remains of the wilderness.

Thirty-five years later, I move into a small apartment in Jerusalem, with a clear unforgiving view of the wadi, Beit Jala in the distance, and sometimes, when the heat haze dissipates, Herodium's flat, cropped head.

The apartment has a small garden. Bare and strewn with pointy dead leaves and olive pits. At the center, the Tree, the culprit. A massive, thickset, arrogant old Levantine that drops its wrinkled fruits like so many farts on the rusty swing chair's corrugated roof.

During the nine months that my presence in this place will last, the nine months that separated me from kibbutz Kfar Avraham, I had the company of the one I'd call alternatively and polyglottally Third'Ear or HaOzen-Hashlishit. An ugly, scrawny, and aggressive kitten, endowed with a third ear, like a pink rhizome in the hollow of his left ear. He was a wild young'un of the garbage, dumpster type, streaked with red, black, and white. The bad boy from a litter of Oriental ragpickers. No shyness, just cunning. No sooner had he arrived than he occupied the left wing of the garden, the side next to the parking space that offers adventurers many possible escapes or hideouts, not least of all the lush verbena plant.

One never really knows why one's good with cats.

I was alone and set on finishing my book by spring, and the presence of this little fella from the wadi gave my undertaking that finishing "cursed-poet-at-work" touch that was not at all unpleasant. People don't realize how eager "the writer" or "the artist" is, even when they are alone, to invent for themselves a decor that puts them in the best light, a vanity theater that lends itself to the flowering of their creative potential. Accordingly, Third'Ear was most welcome.

A bowl under the verbena plant. Some milk with water, morsels of an American brand of tuna, and the fella has it made. Conquest of the garden from east to west, occupation of the battered cushion on the swing chair when it's in the shade. Third'Ear doesn't look down his nose at slivers of schnitzel either.

The very first time he stepped into the apartment, he did so through a slightly ajar window in the kitchen rather than through the wide-open bay window in the living room—a thief, I tell you. I watch him out of the corner of my eye, guardedly discovering the cool tiles, the smell of coffee, cigarettes, and alcohol too.

Once an alley cat, always an alley cat! He disappears for hours on end to hang out with his pals in the parking area, on the edge of the wadi. He's still in his youth, so he chases butterflies and everything that hops and everything that flies and when he comes back home, he heads straight to rest under my bed.

I've never been able to pet him, never even come closer than a yard. Not a trace of gratitude. Affection . . . don't even mention it! He eats, he sleeps where it's cool, he's ugly, he has three ears and unlikely colors and black eyes from the neighborhood thugs. He doesn't trouble himself, not even for a moment, to show any interest in me. At first, on his guard, he gave me a wide berth, but soon enough he understood that I wasn't going to bother him, so he saunters by, tail held high, without a glance, like an effendi on his land. Arrogant as hell!

He has a Pasolinian side to him, this Third'Ear does— a Pasolini, lord of sordid beaches, predation, and solitude. I don't think I've ever written about him. Maizena had the honor of *La Nouvelle Revue Française*; Third'Ear, never. I chose the lady over the tramp.

I know, it's easy, somewhat silly no doubt, but I still wonder why I picked the upper-class lady of my youth over him.

I was wrapping up my novel. My divorce was about to be finalized. It was sometime in February. Raining and very cold. The Japanese oil-burning stove released a sweet smell that reminded me of winters on the kibbutz. Third'Ear had taken over the red Ikea armchair and was watching me finish my book. The olive tree, in the Samaritan wind, was playing Ray Barretto on the roof of the swing chair.

I was going to leave the apartment before the end of the lease, so I was casting about for a new tenant. The spot was pretty, the apartment that I'd furnished with Scandinavian kits was likeable enough to just about anyone, and the winner was a religious newlywed couple. They came with their parents to sign the lease. I made them coffee, we ate the leftovers of a cinnamon cake that had survived Shabbat, and then they saw the cat come in and settle under my desk. The mother asked if he were mine and I said yes. The books went first, by parcel post. I finished packing my suitcases. The sun was already blazing. I didn't really pay attention, but I do believe that it was when I took the last books off the shelves that Third'Ear decided not to come back. The tuna dried under the verbena plant, and I tossed the rest of the milk into the sink.

GIDI'S RETURN

She gave him a black look, her chest heaved under her blue canvas shirt. "You were born here so you're required to present an Israeli passport." She handed his passport back to him with the ugly glare of a bailiff in a rabbinic court.

"This is the only ID I have," he stammered before recalling that, at the bottom of his wallet, folded in two behind an old photo of his daughter when she was three, a stiff sheet of paper had been waiting for twenty years stamped with the number 238357 and the *Tsahal* coat of arms.

After that, he'd had to promise an obese sergeant nearing retirement to stop by the military services and the Ministry of the Interior in Jerusalem within seventy-two hours to regularize his situation. At the end of the interview, the paunchy official in a creased uniform stood up, making an office, whose only amenity was an asthmatic fan, seem smaller still. He held out his hand and, flashing a nicotine-stained smile, said, "welcome home," with a thick Carpathian accent.

As he crossed the tarmac burning from the white sun, he drew a deep breath to fill his lungs with all the violent scents of orange blossom from Lod's orchards. The airport that now bore the name of the nation's founding father had all the characteristics of an airport in a small Southern Californian locality. A motley crowd waited impatiently behind a barrier that three policemen tried rather feebly to maintain.

He gave up on waiting on the line for a bus or for a shared sherut minivan and took a "special" taxi. The driver was a jovial Iraqi with a black velvet kippa held in place by a fluorescent pink clip. He was talkative and Gidi was happy with his chit-chat, a foretaste of the intense inter-rogation that he'd have to face.

"Twenty years in America!" his driver's gaze clouded over, "Not even in '67? Not even for Kippur?"

(Where were you Gidi when your unit fought twice on the Golan without you?)

Not much had changed, except for the size of the cities and their jumble of concrete. A few more palm trees too.

He took a room at the Dan overlooking the sea. The sun set so quickly. He'd forgotten how the uncannily huge sun here would disappear so far west with such haste, as if fleeing, abandoning the city to its flickering urban lights.

He unpacked his suitcase only to find that all the clothing he'd carefully folded two days before in his house in Princeton marked him as a foreigner. What was he thinking he'd do with all these ties and starched shirts? The most suitable thing he had for the local climate was a canvas suit that made him look like a British colonist in the East Indies. The many American tourists in the hotel all wore Hawaiian shirts and looked no sillier than he did in his safari suit with six buttoned pockets, as if to dissuade the young pickpockets in some Third World country. There were a lot of people on the Tayelet, the promenade running south along the seashore to the rock of Jaffa. Opposite the Hassan Bek Mosque, Arab women bathed fully clothed in the shadows. And one could barely see the specks of color floating on the surface of the pitch-black web of mystery and the dark unknown.

It was the same diesel locomotive, the same cars, the same wooden benches for four, the same wooden shudders that took him to Binyamina, the closest station to Kfar Avraham, and one that would have borne comparison with the ones in Tel Aviv or Rutland or Chester in the far reaches of Vermont.

It was a day of khamsin when everything was yellow. At a stand by the station you could buy the newspaper, salted sunflowers seeds, or a hot dog. Gidi felt pity for the sausage with wrinkly skin sitting at the bottom of a jar of lukewarm water. The roll was soggy and covered with small soggy sesame seeds, and the sweet and sour mustard was dry in spots. He ate it with relish as he headed north on the wind- and sun-swept road.

Gidi waited a good half hour before a Peugeot pickup from a neighboring moshav drove him closer to the kibbutz. He took the opportunity to count the eucalyptus and date palms that formed a barrier protecting the orange and banana groves from the biting wind and shards of ice.

He was walking toward the Beit Menashe junction when someone from Kfar Avraham, a girl who must have been his daughter's age, gave him a lift. A bit further down the road, she stopped again to pick up a weary old woman wearing a tight multicolored headscarf who said she was a friend of the writer Dani Armon. It made him smile to think that this old lady, wrinkled as a dried carnation, fingers coarse from detergent and housework, was a friend of the cold, contemplative hermit.

The driver dropped them off in front of the Colbo convenience store that doubled as a post office and station for a bus that stopped, in fact, four kilometers away. The old lady climbed up the hill, following the young driver's directions.

He stood there for a few seconds noting the majestic presence of administrative buildings and the new dining hall. The semicircular shed of corrugated metal was gone, swallowed up by a park with pine trees and a playground.

The single grave where Henia and Avshalom were buried was well kept. A white gravel heart naively decorated the practically yellow stone.

Was it the heat? The fatigue? Gidi fell flat on his nose. His heart heaved in his chest. Suddenly he was cold and his right hand that had done a lousy job breaking his fall pounded with blood.

He woke in the shade of the cypress trees that formed the boundary of the cemetery. Stunned, he got up without difficulty after listening to his own breathing for a few minutes. He placed a stone on the grave, a smooth, perfectly round pink stone that he'd taken with him to America, a stone that Henia had picked up in 1932 on Atlit beach.

WE ARE HEADING INTO FEAR

Zilpa Metzl proposed that I tell her about the day Rabin died.

She knows that the prime minister's assassination on November 4, 1995 was the moment of *shever*, the breaking point, when nearly all the beliefs and certitudes that I'd carried around like medals rattling on my chest collapsed.

I don't think that my view of that day is especially unique. At the time, I was head of the packaging plant for the three Gush Menashe kibbutzim and in charge of recently planted groves.

I was sick that Shabbat—probably with bronchitis again—in any case, it was a Shabbat of fever and rage. I had to give up my plans to go to Kings of Israel Square that evening when the whole peace camp was organizing a huge rally in support of the government and the Oslo Accords.

It had all been arranged. I was supposed to leave for Tel Aviv with Judith and other friends after Shabbat was over. We were planning to meet at the junction to catch a Peach Now chartered bus on its way down from Haifa. And now I had to drop the idea of joining the crowds swelling in the heart of Tel Aviv, and at last witnessing and participating in the rather belated reaction of the left after weeks of rallies of the right and far right, weeks of hatred, shouting, and insults, weeks of rants and diabolical prayers.

Three days earlier, the thickset minister of housing, Binyamin Ben Eliezer, had been attacked on his way to the Knesset in the vicinity of the Rose Garden, Gan HaVradim, by a mob of settlers. On the airwaves of the army station Galei Tzahal, he said he'd seen death in his assailants' eyes. General "Fuad" Ben Eliezer, the hawk in Rabin's government, who'd survived three wars, confessed that he'd been scared. Scared of those Jews, of their madness.

The fury was right there, before our very eyes, plastered all over the walls of the capital, on roads, on bridges, on barbed-wire fences in fields, on balconies.

I had recently visited Jerusalem, which had become a citadel of Messianic nationalist hatred, from Mahane Yehuda market to Pat Junction and from Kiryat Menachem to East Talpiot. A month earlier, the head of the opposition, Benjamin Netanyahu, surrounded by his guard dogs with rotting canines, stood on a terrace in Zion Square exhorting his troops—an unleashed crowd brandishing portraits of

Rabin as an SS officer—and smiling at the chorus of "Death to Rabin" and "Judenrat" chants.

It was all as clear as could be. We had the images and the soundtrack of the tragedy to come, and we were passive and blind.

Rabin became prime minister in 1992 by an unlikely conjunction of stars and planets apparently ignorant of the country's actual sociology. Rabin becoming prime minister was a mistake in casting, a miraculous mistake, but a mistake, nonetheless.

Must we always remember where we were when we heard an exceptional and even catastrophic piece of news? What's the point of knowing where we were when Ben Gurion declared Independence, when Kennedy was assassinated, or when Apollo landed on the moon? To establish our place in history? To integrate our own private story into the bigger picture? To say, that I may not have been there, but I was still here? To insist that I was a contemporary of the events, that I was alive when they happened independently of me, like the totality of what occurs in the universe, that ignores me and that I ignore?

So, here goes. I was in Kfar Avraham that day. I was sick. I remember the weather. It was a lovely evening as it often is in November before the first rains.

But what's the good of remembering what that day shattered in me?

Zilpa wants to know. So, I'll tell her that I was with my three girls who were sleeping over at our home at the kibbutz. I'll tell her that I howled as I watched the images on TV, the nearly silent images. I'll tell her that I woke Judith and the three children who were eleven, seven, and four. I'll tell her that I howled like a wadi jackal, like a leprous wild dog who understands that it will soon have to sever its paw to free itself from the grip of the trap.

What's the good of remembering that day? It always brings back the boundless wave of despair and hatred that engulfed me and took the form of uncontrollable tears.

It wasn't of course the first time that a Jew had killed another Jew, and who knew this better than the attorney Zilpa Metzl. They'd already assassinated Arlosorrof, assassinated Kasztner, assassinated Grünzweig. All those misguided offspring of Pinchas Ben Eleazar, of the zealots, of Jabotinsky, of Kahana.

I'll tell her about all that and about the sudden hatred I felt for a portion of my people, a portion of my people that was no longer my people.

Tamar, the youngest of my girls, had drawn a picture that her cousin Yotam placed by the coffin lying in state in front of the Knesset.

A week spent bawling, I won't lie to Zilpa, a whole week. I'd take my tractor at dawn and would disappear into the groves. I still don't know what I was doing there. Mounir came one afternoon. We shared his tea and my box of cookies among the pomegranate trees.

We cried together, the Arab and the Jew. So that's what I remember of that night and that week. I really don't know what good it does, Zilpa, to talk about all this. More than twenty-five years have gone by, and my anger has only grown, swelling like a horrible tumor. Our hands are dirty. I didn't see, we didn't see the child that Zionism carried in it, starved as we were for justice, redemption, and revenge. We thought we were carrying a New Man, a new emancipated generation as A. D. Gordon claimed, when in fact we were bound, like every human being on this earth, by the violence inherent to humans and to human power. Buber, Magnes, Scholem, and Steiner thought of the Jews as ethical and emancipated; Zionism ultimately imposed on them the banality of humanity and its bondage. We wanted messianic times without the Messiah; they want the Messiah without being worthy of him.

And this scumbag straight from the belly of the most primal and profoundly primitive hatred descended on this people whose ethics and human saga I idealized.

I'd seen the troops of Rehavam "Gandhi" Ze'evi during a patriotic parade down a street in Jaffa. It was the day marking the liberation of Jerusalem. They were goose-stepping, with banners stitched to their bellies, and the general, with his crew cut and his chest held high, was marching in front of his militia. I laughingly told Judith that I was sure his foreskin must have grown back because this man had nothing Jewish about him and everything of a snarling, racist little goy.

Over time I told myself that Zionism had perhaps conceived it all: the stupid messianism of the left, the rancid messianism of the revisionists, the fascist messianism of the settlers, the petty messianism of the ultra-orthodox . . . And I was one of the blind. I was just like all those who hadn't understood that after the February Revolution would come that of October and its sinister procession, just like all those communists who waited for Khrushchev's report, Budapest and Prague for the scales to fall from their eyes, and those even worse scoundrels, who'd stood fast until the collapse of the wall and with it their illusions.

Everything that I'll tell her will serve no purpose and it will not at any rate constitute attenuating circumstances.

For twenty-five years I nursed my hatred like a tree, pruned its dead branches with my red shears, cut back new growth, made the fruit swell to the point of rotting. My attorney Zilpa Metzl will ask me why I waited twenty-five years. I won't be able to tell her about this tree that was growing inside me and was just begging to release its fruit. No one, not even she, will understand this story of the garden of Gehenna. No one, not even Judith, will understand why I went that morning to the beach in Caesarea.

It had taken me two hours on foot. The summer, eager for burns, was already rearing its head. I'd cut across the field and all the burrs of Gush Menashe had clung like pompoms to the bottom of my pants. When I'd reached the road, some idle kids smoking in the shade of a *trempiyada* called me a son of a bitch for no apparent reason except their desire to call someone a son of a bitch.

We were heading into fear, irremediably, into days as gut-churning as an oil slick.

The sun was white on the beach. There were thousands of sharp shells under my feet. Perspiration blurred my vision. I heard the sea lapping gently against the rocks, nibbling away at the belly of the rocks with each caress. And the rocks paid no attention to the sea gnawing at them, corrupting them, stealing their eternal part of eternity.

He was alone on the natural dike that turns the beach into a secluded cove. I couldn't see him clearly because of the white sun and his white hair. His stocky body formed a soft arc between the sky and the rock. I didn't hear what he said to me. The wind, perhaps. I distinctly saw him raise his right hand to greet me, like he greeted his constituents in the Mahane Yehuda marketplace.

It was only when I was about ten meters away that I pulled the trigger.

Givat Ada
February 14, 2020

GLOSSARY

balagan: a mess, chaos.

falh'a: common kibbutz term for field, from the Arabic.

HaAretz: literally "the land," meaning Israel.

Hashomer: a Jewish defense organization in Palestine established in 1909.

Tsahal: Israeli Defense Forces

yishuvim: settlements, plural of *yishuv*.